Recipient

Recipient

By DC Fidler

Published by DCFidler Publishing

2022

Published by DCFidler Publishing
1117 University Avenue, #505
Morgantown, WV 26505
DCFidlerpublishing@gmail.com

Printed in the United States of America
by Kindle Direct Publishing

10, 9, 8, 7, 6, 5, 4, 3, 2

WGAE Registration: 1353214

ISBN: 979-8-9855209-7-2 (paperback)
ISBN: 979-8-9855209-8-9 (ebook)

Appreciation

Thank you to Sandi Constantino-Thompson for your wonderful editing suggestions and your infectious enthusiasm that kept me writing and rewriting long hours each day.

Thank you to RJ Casey and Travis Teffner, my frequent co-writers, who are consistently my audience when I write solo.

Thank you to my wonderful writing teachers: Doris Betts, Max Steele, Wallace Kaufman, and writer-in-residence Robert Anderson at the University of North Carolina at Chapel Hill. That was decades ago, but your caring presences continue to instruct me.

Recipient
By DC Fidler

May 2016

Inside my head is ugly. Unrelenting wars between dreams, imagination, memories and invading demons. Explained by a navy doctor. "Seaman? You have multiple devils dancing in your head." Maybe the doctor said that. Maybe I imagined he said that. Mom claims as a child, I exasperated her making up what she said. "Alton? Your imagination's killing me."

No matter what the doctor said—or I imagined he said—his remaining words got drowned out by chants.

I hear chants. Began when I was five.

Our countrified doctor, chain-smoking while making old-fashioned house calls and farm calls, told Mom I would outgrow the cacophony in my head. Even though Mom was an encyclopedia, we looked up "cacophony" in her heirloom, ragged-cloth dictionary. "A harsh mixture of sounds." I could tell from the manner she rested her hand atop the frayed cover, as if it were a casket lid, the book connected her to people long gone.

For years, chants waxed and waned until fading near the end of high school. Then came me serving in the Navy and a ship magazine exploded. Launched me like a clown catapulted from a circus cannon. Splattered me onto an iron wall, spread-eagle like the coyote in Roadrunner cartoons. Four men—boys really—killed.

My chants returned. Enhanced. Aggressive as if on steroids.

I can't identify the direction of chants. No direction.

Every direction. Sailor-whispered chanties vibrating up my bones into my skull. I won't tell you what my head sailors chant. You would fear me. If I authored those chants, I would fear me. But I'm not author. I'm recipient.

A Veterans doctor once told me, "Rather than thinking of your chants as curses, reframe them as ballads. Gifts. Like music in Mozart's head. God-given gifts." He mimed placing earbuds on his beachball-size head. Earbud music? Mozart, Elton John, Dolly Parton, "Abide with Me," Metallica? Been there, tried that.

I'm twenty-six, but Mom insists accompanying me to VA Hospital visits. She allies with all my doctors. "He's right, Alton honey. Embrace your gift. Don't fight your gift."

I wish the barely-able-to-breathe doctor would have vomited out a word other than "gift." "Gift" is Mom's go-to word. In my younger years, Mom and I were saddled with being poor and surviving a drought. Mom would say, "Alton? Let you and me think of hunger as a gift, creating a threshold for us to cross and treasure future tastes."

There were days, as many as three in a row, food never arrived. "Just think, Alton," she whispered, mussing my hair, "You're going to enjoy your next meal the most."

Then came along a man I was instructed to call "Dad" for seven months as Mom tried to win over the transient but capable mechanic, ogling him like an eighth-grade girl lined up at a school-gym dance, grinning and winking at the school-jock hero. One night, Dad-man jerked me hard—I don't remember for what. He dislocated my four-year-old shoulder, scurrying away as my visiting aunt called the sheriff. Like always, Mom disgusted me with her avalanche of positivity. A disposition tattooed onto her heart by her Baptist-zealot stepmother. In the hospital, she told me, "Alton honey, focus on how much you'll appreciate that shoulder once it heals."

After months and bouts of infection, I did appreciate. To this day, I appreciate my left shoulder more than my right. In grade school, I learned to pitch with either arm. Threw batters off, annoying them enough they called me names. Loudon Ernst was first to scream, "Wacky Aky." I yelled back, "My name's not Aky. It's Alton." My teammates laughed and then spit. Unspoken rule: no accusing, snickering or jeering if you don't spit afterwards. "Wacky Aky" stuck. When batters stepped up to home plate, they hollered, "Show me what you got, Wacky Aky." I complained to my teacher, but Miss Pitts lectured me. "Ignore them. At least that gang of brigands learned their alliteration." I was thankful chants mushroomed during baseball seasons, drowning out yells of "Wacky Aky" from those wannabe-baseball legions. Bunch of losers. Most grew up to become failed farmers. Two in prison. Two gutter drunks. One AWOL. One banker—biggest loser of all. One shuffling house-to-house, peddling vacuum cleaners and electric tooth brushes. I became a plumbing store clerk.

Today is Wednesday. Wednesdays we close at noon like many small-town stores. I visit Hilltop Lanes, a bowling alley with an inside door adjoining Boz's Hilltop Sports Bar. Every Wednesday, Boz pulls me a draft. Corona Light with a lime slice jammed onto the sharp glass edge. I carry my pint glass into the alley, feeling calmed by pins erupting as pot-bellied bowlers scream, "Strike!"

I sit in an unlit row of connected plastic seats on a raised carpeted platform overlooking lane five, one of two center lanes. My usual seat. I sit there if I have the row to myself. If anybody sits nearby, I drink standing behind the seats.

Once, Boz entered, hovered over me, asked if I ever bowl.

"Nope."

"So why come here? You don't talk to nobody."

I raised my glass in a toast to him. "Don't like to drink alone."

He looked funny at me, approached Lois, renting shoes and lanes, and exchanged a handful of twenties for smaller denominations. He whispered something while Lois assured Andrew Jackson faced upward on each twenty. Symmetry. Boz nodded at me with gritted teeth. Lois shrugged and shook her head as if saying, "poor schmuck." To hell with them. I don't need their pity.

Months ago, I tried a bar three blocks away. College types and business types with money. Ties. Fancy beers. No Corona Light. I didn't like coffee or chocolate or whatever contaminated their beer. Polo-shirt people stared as I sucked off foam. Chants grew louder. After three sips, I fled.

"Whacky Aky." Some days, I hear Loudon Ernst holler that. A memory from our grade-school ballfield. But I'm not trying to recall it, so, that's not a memory, right? I think a demon is pulling a moment from nowhere and stuffing it into my head. In the tenth grade, a drunk driver ran down Loudon in our school crossing. I didn't attend his funeral. Maybe he's the demon, returning to torture me.

Today, a foursome of two construction fellas and their dates, wives, girlfriends are laughing too loud. No rings on fingers. They're conquering lane five. High two-hundreds. One woman in a red-striped dress is sitting it out. She's ultra-pregnant. I bet her belly button popped out like my cousin's did when she was carting cantaloupe breasts and a watermelon belly. I wonder how much it hurts, having an inside creature stretching you into an overinflated balloon, knowing something may crawl out of you any moment. She's sweating lots. Shifting positions. Mom would say, "Guess one day she'll treasure having a normal human belly." I can see that. Able to cross her legs. Roll a bowling ball. Have sex. Maybe she still has sex. How in God's name? I wish I hadn't thought that. Now, I want to ask her. How would I begin such a conversation? "Nice red-striped maternity dress. Oh, by the way." Her guy would probably punch me out. Like when I asked a wheelchaired airman if rolling his "adult tricycle" built up his biceps. His brother or friend laid me out. Chipped an upper center tooth. Now I whistle when I talk.

On days chants are especially mean, I bite my lime. Sour tastes tame chants a moment. The reason I sometimes ask Boz for two slices. When I do, he frowns. I can tell he wants to charge for extra lime, but I never offer. His glare proves he thinks bad of me. I would never hurt him. Not even when chants say so.

June 2016

I yearn for Saturday afternoons. Just like Wednesdays, Potts Brothers Plumbing closes midday. Every Saturday, I hike across barren farm fields, passing charred ruins of Pap-pap's farm house and barn where Dad grew up. Kid vandals set fire to them.

I shoot rusted tin cans from a twenty-four-year-old scrap pile. No cans added since 1992 when Dad disappeared during a Colombian jungle mission. I was two. My only Dad memory is playing with a toy gun, Dad dramatically dying repeatedly on Mom's spiral throw rug when I pointed my finger and screamed, "Bang."

Pablo Escobar was killed the following year. Shot through the ear while trying to escape crawling across his roof. Only I know who shot that drug lord. Government coverups. Dad's hiding out on special missions. Mom doesn't know. I protect her from such pain.

Seven cans. Always shoot seven. My lucky number.

Time to move on to bigger game. Melons and cantaloupes. The cantaloupes are overly ripe. Deserve what's coming. Cantaloupe one explodes orange goo after a three-round burst. Easy. Eight Saturdays ago, I missed. I pounded my scalp enough to draw blood. I deserved that. Wherever Dad is, he was disappointed. Nothing worse than disappointing fathers.

Cantaloupe two. On target. Loupe three. On target. Loupe four. Quarter-inch off center. Blew up but below promised standards. Slight wind. I know how to accommodate wind. No forgiveness. Cantaloupe five. On target. Loupe six. Loupe seven.

Now watermelons. They slosh pink. Blood red when ripe. The biggest girl sounded ripe when I thumped her. A sound hard to describe. A sound Pap-pap taught me to recognize before his dementia. I was six. A fast learner. My grandpa misbelieved he could predict my life. "Alton, you're gonna make a most amazing farmer. Your dad would have too if he hadn't settled for a different life." The word "settled" didn't sit well with me. Farmers feed the world. Soldiers protect that world. Without soldiers, there is no farming. Pap-pap never served. Worse, he never expressed gratitude to his two brothers for making his world safe. God punishes the selfish with dementia. Pap-pap died not knowing he was dying. Died not remembering I was his only grandchild, named to inherit his fallen farm.

I sight the biggest watermelon. Dark green stripes on a putrid green background. Select the center stripe. Wait for wind to lull. Hold for silence. An image of the bowling-alley woman. Her lumbering watermelon belly and white maternity dress with red stripes. Same colors as targets. Pick the center stripe. With each breath, the red stripe moves outward and retreats. Wait for the stripe to be outward. I am one with my target, unable to feel my weapon. The watermelon explodes, spraying rich chunks of juicy organs.

The echo dies.

A murder of crows abandons its viewing stand, announcing celebratory success to nearby forest animals.

Mission accomplished. Time to relax. Lie on my back. Enjoy one puffy cloud shading me for the moment. The world at peace.

Dad is chuckling like he did falling on Mom's throw rug. Bang.

July 2016

Eleven o'clock before my first customer stumbles in, dangling a small chain hooked to a black rubber stopper. "Water leaks outta my bathroom sink."

People never realize how naked they are, standing before me, revealing house-plumbing problems. The stopper's edge is frayed and caked with decades of soap oils and traces of rust. What else in his house has been neglected? Door thresholds? Window seals? Oven grills? When's the last time he looked under his hood and cleaned his engine? Checked his car's oil or window-washer fluid? What about personal hygiene? Does he scrub his underarms? Wash between his toes? Clean his balls? He smiles and I see his teeth. No way he'll own his gray teeth much longer.

"What color stopper do you want?"

"Color?"

"Black? White? Ivory?"

"Oh. Same. Black."

He follows me to aisle three.

I examine sizes on the small boxes as I grill him. "I haven't seen you in here before."

"I usually shop College Street Mall. Walmart. Home Depot. But it's a twenty-three-mile drive. I only need one little stopper." He glances around. "You have quite the inventory."

"Everything big stores carry. And then some."

"Huh. I'll have to remember that."

He won't. He'll combine grocery shopping with hardware shopping with pharmacy shopping with filling up his SUV tank with grabbing a donut and coffee. I listen to his breathing. A mouth breather. Dries the throat. Smelly bacteria grow. Bet his wife hates kissing him.

Holds her breath and quickly pulls away.

"Does your wife like having a black stopper?"

That threw him for a loop. "Never asked her. She'll go with whatever I pick."

I bet he picks everything for the two of them. Orders her around. Like the bossy man Mom seduced into our home when I was four. The one who dislocated my shoulder.

"Here you go. Black stopper with hanging ring. Anything else?"

"Nope."

"Feel free to look around."

"I got all I need."

I bet that's his attitude with sex too. "I got all I need." Doesn't matter if his wife wants something more. An extra kiss. Lying together and quietly hugging. Whispering sweet talk to one another. "I got all I need."

"How much?"

"Two-twenty-two."

"Wow. That's cheap. You'd have to sell a shitload of stoppers to pay rent for this big ole building."

"1922."

"Huh." He pulls out a tarnished money clip and flips through bills. No particular order. Presidents and founding fathers not facing the same direction. Figures.

He forks over a Lincoln. "Why's there a vintage Esso gas pump out front?"

"This used to be a general store. Mr. Potts likes preserving a few mementos. There's an old pot-bellied stove and a wall of gold-trimmed mailboxes out back."

"You don't say. Regular museum."

I give him his two-seventy-eight change.

"No tax?"

"Mr. Potts pays the tax. Says figuring out charging customers tax is a waste of time."

"Huh."

"Need a bag?"

He stuffs the boxed stopper into his coat pocket.

"Nope."

I walk to the dozens of window panes framed in 1922 oak and watch him drive away. His black SUV is coated in dried mud. Hard as concrete after drying for weeks or months.

I wish his wife well.

I wonder where they live. In town? On a pretend farm? City slickers are fast buying up nearby farms but not farming. Museum pieces to brag about to their urban-prisoned friends.

I write down his license-plate number. It will be easy to locate this fella and his wife.

August 2016

Mom announced her sister Adele in Tampa requires hip surgery. Aunt Adele lives alone, so Mom will visit and nurse her six weeks. Mom refuses to fly, claiming Dad likely died in a helicopter blown from the sky. Although she'll never admit it, Mom has an unhealthy imagination. One of my VA doctors, don't remember his name, VA doctors being as replaceable as car batteries, told me, "All of us are paranoid some. Folks hear a siren and think police is ambushing 'em. Ponder what's in hotdogs. But some folks are profoundly paranoid. Know why?"

I shrugged.

"They see the world too clearly. Can't deny reality like most folks. Fixate all this land we cherish is riding atop molten lava. And such shit."

Mom'll take a bus to Raleigh and transfer in Atlanta to some Florida bus.

Although weekdays I ride my bike a mile to Potts Brothers, and Saturdays seven miles to the farm, Mom handed over keys to her 2006 Prius for grocery trips. Back in 2014, when I renewed my license, Mom appeared amazed. "You were able to renew your license?" I explained DMV examiners inquire about vision, seizures, ability to interpret road signs, traffic violations, drug and alcohol use, residency. No inquiry about chants. She raised her eyebrows, yanked her car keys from the hall hook, and zipped them in her purse.

Last night, Mom wrote out recipes. I rarely cook but those look easy. She stuffed cash in the Oreo cookie jar. Money for gas, water, electric, cable, phone bills. I didn't tell her I plan to camp in the hunting cabin hidden in the woods on my farm. I doubt she remembers it exists. No electricity or running water but cozy. More my style.

She showed me Aunt Adele's photo. Grown too old to recognize.

Mom wanted to buy a cell phone for me to keep in touch. I declined. U.S. government traces cell phones. The signal would disclose my cabin.

Dad can locate me. The cabin will be the first place he'll check. Pap-pap said Dad used to camp there and drink Kentucky bourbon with his best friend, Arch. Arch is an Air Force PJ. I met him once when he visited Pap-pap. I was twelve. Arch said I was the spitting image of my dad down to the mole on my left ear. He hugged me. I didn't hug back. I liked he smelled of military canvas.

I'll cart a few of Mom's books to the cabin. As a girl, she desired to teach literature at a university, but "settled" for being a Special Force's wife. Later, kept us afloat selling Hallmark cards and little stuffed animals. Back when people wrote instead of texting like I see patrons at Boz's bar.

When Mom was teaching me to read, she engrossed me reading aloud. *Great Expectations* and *Last of the Mohicans.* As a teen, she read me *War and Peace* and *Beowulf.* She not only read; she performed characters. Absolutely different voices for each person or creature. Even varying voices for the different sections of prose. Those special moments silenced my chants. In school, teachers read *Harold and the Purple Crown* and *If You Give a Mouse a Cookie.* Caused my chants to roar. I would excuse myself, not explaining my abrupt exit. Of course, that resulted in detention.

Mom made her bus on time, after guilting me into getting her to the BP-service-station bus stop an hour early. "You act like you wish me to be late. Do you hate my sister that much?" I barely remember Aunt Adele. Certainly not the wilted lady in Mom's photo. A myriad of lines crisscrossing her witch face, shouting a history similar to tortured women I overhear in Boz's bar. "I'm a person who needs lots of support." "I get stressed easily." "I could never survive going through what she did." "I'm very aware of myself." "I'm nobody without him." "I still say you should leave him."

When I ride my bike to my farm, I don't have to worry about hitchhikers. No way to pick them up. But today, driving Mom's Prius? I can offer a ride. But would a hiker appreciate a seven-mile lift? Would a hiker become violent if I stopped and interrupted him from landing a ride going greater distance? Would a hiker carjack me? Would I pick up a hiker and immediately fall in love? I overheard a shopper at Potts Brothers spin a yarn about such. Dated a woman hitchhiker several months. But when she learned he wasn't worth millions, she broke his nose with her shoe, the high heel barely missing his eye. He was a slug. Dragged his feet. Pap-pap taught me, people who slide their feet across floors and ground think nothing of their own worth. I pick up my feet. Walk with left and right feet strictly parallel. Efficient. Silent. Like lions approaching grazing prey. Native Americans stalking game. Snipers tailing marks.

I pass two teenage girls hitchhiking. Cutoff jean shorts revealing too much. In my rearview mirror I see a semi stop. Too heavy to pull onto the soft shoulder. Blocks the road. I surveil the girls jog and climb up into the cab. I don't want to think more about that.

I out-distance the truck and swerve onto my farm's dirt road. All gravel disappeared years ago, washed away by spring deluges. Thick trees and undergrowth provide impenetrable walls, an occasional oak or maple limb shaking hands with the opposite side.

The road ends in an open field. No way a Prius can traverse hundred-year-old troughs and mounds and knotted vines and red-clay clods. I'll have to hike back and forth a half-dozen times with provisions. I cackle as I imagine Mom saying, "Be sure to take a roller suitcase with you, honey." Yeah. Right.

Fourth trip, I panic upon return to the Prius. It's locked. I don't remember locking it. I can't find Mom's keys. House and car and lockbox keys on one of Dad's old key rings, attached with a stretchy coil to a plastic Minnie Mouse. How could I lose a ridiculously colorful piece of junk? Stupid.

Sweat oozes up and out my shirt collar as a rush of blood sears my face. I dropped the fucking keys. Didn't I clip Minnie to my belt? I'm sure I did. The conglomeration of plastic and metal could be under leaves or vines or anywhere along the half-mile trek. I pat my pockets seven times. Wait a minute. My cargo pockets at knee level. I never stuff anything but ammo in those pockets. Shit. I feel a bulge. Oh, please God. Don't be ammo. Be keys.

Through the canvas, I feel Minnie's oversized ears. I pull her into the light. Yes! I sit on a mound, waiting for heartbeats to slow. Beats refuse to cooperate. What happened to the short-short girls? Did Mom transfer buses or get left behind in a Raleigh restroom? Did Mom fill the gas tank or run the Prius near empty as usual? Slow down thoughts. Slow down heart. They refuse. Throw a rock. That would feel good. Throw a rock so hard it digs a hole in earth. The chants sing, "Do it. Do it."

I obey.

Early September 2016

After work, I stop at Mom's to heat a can of beef stew. She left a message on the world's last answer machine. Aunt Adele needs her an extra three weeks. Maybe they're having fun. Seems doubtful. Women their age with afflicting conditions. But they laugh during phone calls, giggling like school girls. Giggling enough that Mom snorts.

Having Mom's Prius, I'm itching to travel. There's Oreo jar money plus a bonus Mr. Potts gave me. Harmon, a teen boy subbing at Potts, spun tales of camping in the mountains. Pisgah National Forest. Bragged about a deep gorge and giant waterfall. Showed me a photo on his cell phone. He's sitting on a rock protruding out past a cliff, dangling his legs above a fourteen-hundred-foot-deep valley. I asked, "Did you get queasy scooting out to the edge? Rocks can come loose."

"Nope. Them rocks are one-point-two billion years old. Only the moon's got older rocks. That beauty ain't going nowhere. Besides, I hang-glide off Grandfather Mountain." He explained that was close to the gorge. "But Grandfather ain't wilderness. Got lodges and golf courses."

He boasted Green Berets—same as Special Forces— trained in mountain survival in the gorge in the 60s and 70s.

Mr. Potts has a ton of old maps. I looked up Linville Gorge. Roads abruptly end at a large green area labeled, "Wilderness." No secondary or dirt roads.

In Mom's attic is Dad's army-green locker. I open it for the first time in a decade. Years-old dusty air attacks my lungs and makes me cough. Army wool blankets. Sleeping bag. Two shelter halves to hook together to make a tent.

World War Two relics of Dad's uncles. Canteen. Old metal first aid kit and a newer discolored plastic one. Winkler dagger with both edges sharpened. A Winkler hammer combat axe. Binoculars. Repelling rope. Wool socks. Rucksack. Dad's uncles' dog tags. Whetstone. Special Forces olive-green t-shirts. Combat pants with ten pockets. I counted them.

Doorbell rings. Could be a UPS package. Maybe young Mormon guys in white shirts and black ties, scrubbed squeaky clean with abrasive soap. Or a scam artist. I ignore it. The bell rings again. What the hell? I hurry down steps three at a time.

I retract Mom's sheers and peep through a side-window panel. A Girl Scout. Alone. Cookies in September? I don't know. Mom buys Thin Mints and Caramel deLites every year. I retract the sheers farther. Don't see a parent car. The girl's gripping a small pink wagon's handle, hauling a half-dozen boxes and a clipboard. Seven merit badges sewed on her sash. No dog with her. Dogs don't like me. Maybe they hear my chants.

She rings a third time and I crack open the door. "Yes?"

"Hi. I'm Bethany Steiner. Live three blocks over on Sugar Maple Trail. I'm selling Girl Scout cookies. The nice woman of the house bought a magazine subscription from me in April."

I mumble through the door crack, "My mother. I didn't know Girl Scouts sell magazines."

"For a school drive." She steps back and looks me over. I narrow the door opening, but she continues talking. "We were raising money for our band. I play the trombone."

"Trombones are large instruments. You're small."

"I'm strong. I beat my brother arm wrestling."

"Younger brother?"

"Older."

I open the door wider. "Mom's out of state. Florida."

"You can buy cookies."

"Are you alone?"

"My parents are at work. I only have a little bit of time to sell between school and track practice."

"Busy schedule."

"It's healthy to be busy."

"How much for your cookies?"

"Five dollars a box."

"Guess I could buy one."

"If I sell two, I'll qualify for a group bus trip to Fright Farm for Halloween. The sale ends tonight and this is my last house."

"Why did you save us to last?"

"I tried all week. Nobody's been here."

"Oh. Yeah. I've been staying out at my farm. Let me check if I have ten dollars. You can wait in the living room."

"We're not permitted to enter houses."

"Oh."

She stares unwavering at me with no shyness, like a drill sergeant sizing up recruits, and asks, "Why do you have sad eyes?"

I blink hard like someone grabbed me from behind. "I have sad eyes?"

"They're nice sad eyes."

Am I being hit on by a Girl Scout? I want to slam the door. Halt her invasion, but I stand my ground. "Why do you think my eyes are sad?"

"I'm good at seeing into people."

"How old are you?"

"Eleven."

"You look nine."

"Eleven."

"Okay then. Let me test you. When you look at me, what do you see?"

"Someone who is kind. Someone with something eating away inside. Thoughts that won't let go."

I eye her while she evaluates the beef-stew stain on my shirt. I confront her. "You're unusual."

"I was born unusual. Unusual people have to be careful not to make other people uncomfortable."

"Maybe you're making me uncomfortable."

"No. Making you curious. You understand because you're unusual."

"Unusual how?"

"You worry if you think bad, you are bad. But you're not. Goodness depends on what you do."

I pause to ponder if that is generally true for all people. "That's something you could say to every human and be correct. Like something you read on a Hallmark card."

"No. It was for you. Do you want to buy two boxes of cookies or not? I don't have much time."

"I'm deciding."

"You can do it. Just do it. Do it."

My heart begins racing and I try to hide I'm sweating. "Why did you say that? Those exact words?"

She shrugs, never breaking eye contact.

I fetch fifteen dollars and purchase three boxes. She only has three types left. S'mores, Shortbreads, and Lemon-Ups. I buy one of each. Instead of thanking me, she looks at our address, writes it on her clipboard papers, and tows her pink wagon away.

I sit in the kitchen. Should I open a box? Which flavor? I've never heard of any of these. I don't like cookies. But maybe these flavors taste good. Lots of people buy them.

I clutch the Lemon-Ups box. One cookie could be okay. Maybe not.

The chants sing, "Do it. Do it."

I have no choice.

Mid-September 2016

Most cabin days, I boil water in a pot dangling in my fireplace and sponge steaming liquid over my body. But today, I yearn for a shower spicket blasting the hottest water a human body can tolerate. I drive to Mom's. I ignore the dozen yellow stick'ems on her front hall mirror and the dozen duplicates on my bedroom door. But brushing my teeth, it's impossible to ignore yellow assailants glaring at me from my bathroom mirror.

"VA appointment Tuesday Sept. 13 at 2 pm." There are two stick'ems screaming that at me. The second stick'em is lavender. Mom's way of yelling more than once from afar.

Alternating sitting and pacing in the general medical waiting room, I study a soldier in Marine uniform sitting with a woman resting her head on his shoulder. When his name is called, he abandons her. She pouts and stuffs her feet beneath her butt on the couch cushion. What kind of adult does that? How does she know she hasn't stepped in dog shit? She's huddles up like a three-year-old. Maybe she doesn't want to be an adult. Hiding from a world full of harm. I want to approach her and announce life will be okay, but her shrunken posture signals a warning like erect quills on a porcupine. She shrinks into a ball of flesh and cloth, her head tucked as if withdrawn into a turtle shell.

My name is called. I keep my distance passing by the intertwined human.

Doctor Worth is not wearing a white coat or tie. He's sporting one of his many crewneck sweaters. A physician gone undercover. The interrogation begins. "What most attracts you to stay out at your cabin?"

I shrug but answer. "Dad used to camp there with his friend Arch."

"You told me your dad's friend once visited you."

I play ignorant. "I did?"

"When you were twelve."

He slipped. Gave away that he files notes of my every word. I once told him his questions remind me of undercover agents and he replied, "Searching out truths."

I am a game for him, but he's not the best of spies. He's incapable of smoking out what truly resides in my head.

He leans forward with hands clasped beneath his chin, elbows resting on air. "Do you feel closer to your dad when you're in the cabin?"

"No more than anywhere else."

"So … he's always with you."

I shrug. I know he translates my shrugs as unspoken agreement.

His eyes fall from focus as he slides into his own brain. "I lost my twin brother Doug. When we were fourteen."

Long pause but I cling to silence.

His eyes fix on me. "My brother Doug's always with me. Like your father is always with you." His voice is soft, breathy, like Mom's minister at funerals saying, "Sorry for your loss." Faked grief.

That's another spy technique. Mirroring. I once heard a student nurse on the psych ward explain mirroring to her colleague. "Make patients believe you understand, act like you feel their feelings."

Perhaps Worth actually lost his twin brother, but more likely, he's mirroring. Whether his tricks are for my good or my demise, his tricks are deceitful.

"I believe you told me that similar to your dad, his friend, Arch—that was his name, right? Arch?"

I just told this man Dad's friend is named Arch. He's asking in order to fake uncertainty. I nod.

He returns my nod. More mirroring.

"And you told me Arch was also military."

I don't remember sharing that fact. Is he reading my mind? Hearing my chants? I force-think something else. The Girl Scout selling cookies. Her pink wagon. I picture that and wait.

He waits.

He doesn't ask about the girl or cookies or wagon. Maybe in a previous session, I did tell him about Dad's friend. I'll play along. "He's a PJ."

"Who's a PJ?"

"The guy you inquired about. Dad's friend Arch."

"What's a PJ?"

I smirk. Worth's wearing a military ring. He good and well knows what PJs are. He's playing stupid to throw me off. I play along. "PJs parachute from planes and helicopters to rescue people. Rescue Navy Seals and Special Forces behind enemy lines. Rescue civilians trapped in hurricanes."

"Parachuting. Huh." He frowns a moment. "Freefall?"

"HALO. High altitude low opening. Often nighttime. Land in oceans. SCUBA to final destinations. Trained in languages of enemies."

"Huh." His mind wheels are spinning. "James Bond type danger."

I remain still, straining to not reveal he just insulted Arch and his brothers, hoping my face doesn't betray my revulsion.

I journey into my own head, the crew-sweatered doctor and his armed, straight-back leather chair dissolving to nothing as I recall military events as clearly as when I daydream by my cabin fire.

I am on my feet in back of a Chinook lined up to jump, staring out the open rear door at the cargo ramp. Two guys jump, but the third guy plops his ass down on the ramp edge and freezes, refusing to jump, blocking the remainder of us.

Doctor Worth jars me back into his office. "Where has your mind wandered?"

"What?"

"You look like you went deep into your head."

"Oh … uh." I'm trembling. "One day, there was this guy who wouldn't jump. Sat down on the ramp. The jumpmaster punched him in the back with a pole, knocked him off the ramp. Instead of enjoying his freefall, his face was that of someone falling to his death."

"You could see his face as he fell?"

"Uh … yeah … enough."

"So, this is a memory?"

"Yes sir."

The doctor stares out the window a moment as sweat beads roll off my chin and sweat floods my armpits.

He turns to me. "I thought you were a seaman. A mechanic."

I shiver. I want to be back in my cabin, curled in my fireside blanket. "Yes sir. Seaman. Mechanic."

"So … Perhaps rather than being a memory of something you did—saw—you are remembering a story Arch told you. When he visited you. When you were twelve."

"No sir," is on the tip of my tongue. But all I can do is stutter. "It was my … my … my …"

I flee Doctor Worth's office.

Late September 2016

I stop for gas and directions in Linville. The young lady with blond and pink hair behind the counter huffs when I interrupt her absorption with her cell phone. She instructs me, "Most people pay at the pump."

"I don't have a credit card."

"Whatever." She grimaces at me like I'm an alien who gassed up his spaceship. She glances at dials on the wall. "Twenty-three fifty-two."

She stares at the two twenties and two pennies that I plop on a rubber counter mat advertising Winston cigarettes.

"What are the two pennies for?"

"So, you'll give me two quarters instead of a bunch of small change."

She rolls her eyes and slides the pennies back to me, giving me the change amount flashing on her computerized register. Guess her school doesn't teach math.

Dare I ask? I do. "Which way is Linville Gorge?"

"Your phone GPS will give you directions."

"I don't have a cell phone."

"Like really?"

"Like really."

She gestures with an open palm to the right. "Somewhere that way. Stop and ask somebody else when you get closer."

"I thought this was closer."

She huffs again.

I bite my upper lip and leave, thirsting for a Cheerwine, but not wanting more huffs and eye rolls.

Fifteen minutes later, I arrive in Linville Falls, a small crossroads at the junction of three counties. I stare for a moment, amazed that a tavern straddles all three counties. I enter and spot a fellow on the floor tinkering with an ice machine. According to a line on the floor, his torso is in one county and his legs in another.

"Pardon me. Can you point me to Linville Gorge?"

He sits up. "It's close enough to bite you in the ass." He chuckles and points across the street. "Two-thousand feet thataway. The paved road curves, but keep straight on the dirt road. If you're looking for the falls, just a few hundred feet's a parking lot on the left."

"I'm hoping to see the deep part of the gorge. The part with high cliffs."

"Cliffs, huh? Continue on the dirt road four miles to Wiseman's View. Hope your vehicle's eager to bounce over ruts. No help out there if you rupture anything underneath, blow a gasket, get a flat. Happens lots. Truck or car?"

"Prius."

"Then son, I wish you my best." He resumes repairing, making me feel like people all day must pester him for directions. I keep straight on the dirt road, passing Linville Falls parking, and navigating along a trail-like passage that makes troughs and mounds on my farm seem tame. I guess to maintain "wilderness," locals don't desire paved or gravel roads emboldening hordes of tourists.

I hear my undercarriage scrape three times, but treading slowly, the sound resembles slow scraping metal rather than hard hits.

I pass no vehicles coming or going. I do spot a trailer camper sitting in a shallow turnoff. No people. Multiple signs warning to beware of bears.

It takes me thirty minutes to bump along the four miles. A sign announces "Wiseman's View." There's a parking lot with one vehicle, a Land Rover, and beyond the lot is an outhouse. I am in great need of an outhouse before I grab my rucksack and follow the foot trail to the overlook. As Harmon described, from Wiseman's I see Table Rock and Hawksbill jutting skyward from an opposite quartzite wall, towering above the fourteen-hundred-foot-deep gorge. I walk to a patch of moss conquering a granite outcrop, maintaining my distance from the stone threshold of death. Just like Harmon's cell-phone photo, an endless virgin forest flanks a zigzagging river. I don't have a camera. I should have taken Mom up on her offer for a cell phone. But storing this view in my head is all I need.

I hear small rocks crunching on granite. Almost out of view is a man sitting on the edge, much like Harmon did. He's gazing down at the river, up at the sky, back down at the river.

I search for other people. None.

Perhaps this guy can answer my questions.

In no time at all, the man, named Will, is flaunting knowledge about this magical canyon. "It used to be inhabited by Cherokee tribes who called it, 'Ee-see-oh,' for 'River of many cliffs.' Later purchased by John D. Rockefeller. Like much of American wilderness, at one time it was owned by one single rich oil person."

I ease closer to the edge. I can't help but ask. "Do people ever jump?"

Will appears sad. "Yes. People jump. People fall. Flatlanders aren't used to heights, so when they see this high terrain, they immediately realize they could jump if they choose. Their own urges scare the shit out of them." He mumbles under his breath, "Flatlanders."

Before I can censor myself, I blurt out, "They should learn to skydive. Controlled falling."

Will eyes me with an admiring grin. "You skydive?"

"PJ," slips out of my mouth.

"No shit! That's impressive. Was it scary? I mean, on your first jump."

"Actually ... relaxing."

"I always thought it would be."

"You don't sense falling. Just wind rushing by like sticking your head out a car window."

He's hooked on my story. Like Mom used to hook me.

"And you're totally swimming. But in air instead of water. And if you HALO jump—way high up with oxygen, thirty-four-thousand feet or so—you can't even tell you're getting closer to earth. You're floating."

"Freakin awesome."

"It is." Suddenly, I feel sad. I don't know why. Maybe because I'm not floating. Forced to accept I'm stuck down here on earth assuring my oil pan and tail-pipe don't scrape. Trying to get two quarters instead of a handful of small change. But I look out across the gorge and suddenly I'm above worrying. I'm floating.

"Look," Will says, pointing into the gorge. "Peregrine Falcons."

We watch two birds of prey soaring below us.

I can't conceal my elation. "I've never looked down on birds flying before. Just up."

"Rattlesnakes are stuck down there slithering over rocks. Chipmunks scampering over logs. Meanwhile, these two creatures are swimming in wind like you described. And can swim the air at two-hundred miles an hour. Maybe we'll see them catch something."

"Like what?"

"These raptors mostly dine on medium-sized birds."

"Catch them midair?"

"Absolutely. And ground game. Before you came, there was a third falcon. Dive-bombed a river rock and hauled off a squirming squirrel."

"Wow. I hope I get to see that. But I want to see one catch another bird."

We watch together in silence. No need to talk more and lessen the spectacles before us.

After a bit, I want to ask him if a place like this makes people feel more normal. But I don't want to raise suspicion that I'm unusual.

"Well … time for some repelling," he says, and walks to a coiled rope near the edge. I had neither noticed the rope nor appreciated he was wearing gloves. Yellow gloves missing finger tips. I guess to free fingers for climbing back up.

He lifts a harness dangling with assorted-color metal clips, slips into the contraption, and places an unusual helmet on his head. He circles the rope around a boulder and tosses the two loose ends into the canyon. He clips his harness to the ropes and with no "so long" or "wish me luck," he leaps backwards off the cliff.

The two rope strands jerk taut.

All is quiet except a breeze breathing in and around my soft-skin ear folds as sun toasts my face and bare arms.

I wonder how far he jumped. How far he will descend. He's alone. What if he gets stuck climbing back up? Or will he stop on a ledge and hike back up?

The cliff perimeter is luring me to peer over. But what if a blast of wind comes out of nowhere? What if I stumble like I did in the mall, bruising my elbow, but this time no polished marble floor catching me?

I sit by the parallel strands of rope, my legs crossed, my back erect like Native American chiefs in movies sit smoking peace pipes. War pipes. Whatever they smoke.

Maybe when Will reaches bits of rock poking out enough to stand on, the rope will slack and tighten again when he swings out.

But it remains taut.

I hear a falcon call. Could be informing the other it is going in for a kill.

Maybe I can feel Will's movements. I lay two fingers across a rope strand, and then lightly press my fingertips as if checking a pulse. I sense faint vibrations, but maybe because that's what I desire to feel.

How far down is he? Maybe this cliff is a hundred feet. Maybe five hundred. High enough to be a fifty-story building. But nothing near as high as freefall.

The two rope strands are stretched across earth as if they are giant violin strings strung on granite. Perhaps where the rope loops around the boulder, vibrations are more perceptible.

I crawl toward the boulder, but crawling hurts my knees. I half-stand, pleading with wind not to grab me. When I was young, a squall blew me off a South Carolina beach pier, so, I don't trust wind and height. Except skydiving. Freefall wind is liberating. But Doctor Worth said my memory could be Arch's story. What if it is?

No.

It was my memory.

I remember the soldier's face when the jumpmaster forced him off the ramp. Unlike my brothers looking elated as they floated with arms and legs spread, cheeks puffing with waves of skin wiggling as rapid air distorted their faces, the hesitant jumper flailed his arms, his feet searching for a staircase that eluded him. His eyes stretched open as wide as apples are round. Bet he was thinking, "I don't wanna die. Please God not now." But he wasn't screaming. Fear froze his vocal cords. And then his chute deployed and he slowly descended. But incapable to regain control over his panic. Not paying attention to rapidly approaching ground, he crushed bones in one ankle. But he felt no pain as he lay in mud, still consumed by premonitions of dying.

How would Will fare during freefall? Would he enjoy his ride or be imprisoned by fear?

The cliff is no match for the altitude of HALO or even freefall flights. Closer to static-line-jump heights, but still shorter. Briefer rides. Inadequate time to think.

I kneel by the boulder and study the rope.

It seems like the rope would wear from being looped around a boulder and stretched across granite. Especially wearing where it plunges over the granite's jagged edge, rope fibers shredding from the weight of a dangling body aiding the canyon's razor-sharp lip to saw the rope.

The jumpmaster used a pole to shove the reticent jumper. Would Will be reticent? Insist on being roped? Not allowing himself thrills of freefall?

I closer examine the section of looped rope.

Maybe if I slide my Winkler dagger blade between the boulder and rope, the hard-plastic handle will amplify vibrations and I'll hear what Will is doing. Swinging out over the gorge. Swinging side to side. Pausing to enjoy the view. Talking to airborne falcons.

I retrieve my dagger from my rucksack and slide the blade tip behind the rope. The rope is tightly strangling the boulder. I have to apply pressure to wiggle the tip between rope and stone.

Success.

I lie on rock and press my ear against the hard-plastic handle, hoping the dagger performs like a stethoscope. Transmitting sound like when Dawson Meeks and I placed our ears in openings of paper cups strung together with string to make primitive telephones. Placed our ears on railroad tracks to hear approaching trains clicking along. Using our imaginations to picture what activities the sounds were hinting.

Am I hearing Will moving or my own heart beating?

A rhythm of slow beats. A rhythm of slow backstrokes while floating in the ocean, unbreaking waves gently lifting and lowering my limp body. Floating. Up. Down. Up. Down. A rhythm of falcons soaring in canyon winds. Left. Right. Higher. Lower.

I embrace the rhythm. But what is the source?

What is the rope speaking to me? Commanding me to hear?

The rope's vibrations match the rhythm of my chants.

"Do it. Do it."

Do what?

I sit up and see that my double-edged dagger frayed the rope. But only the tiniest bit. A couple of fibers poking out like poorly combed hair. Not enough Will would notice.

"Do it. Do it."

Do what?

Enjoy picturing Will swinging and climbing like he loves?

Something more?

Will considering freefall?

"Do it. Do it."

He's not high enough to have time to embrace air time.

"Do it. Do it."

The dagger is severely sharp. When I first discovered it, I had Pap-pap sharpen it in his tool shop. He demonstrated he was able to slice grilled steak by simply resting his pinkie on the dagger tip.

"Do it. Do it."

I cease feeling for vibrations and crawl away from the boulder to where the strands are stretched across smooth, flat stone. Waiting for me, as if posed upon a cutting block.

"Do it. Do it."

I look to the sky. The place where strength and answers perch, waiting to be summoned.

"Do it. Do it."

"Quiet," I whisper. "I want the sky to speak."

"Do it. Do it."

I shout, "Shut up!"

"Do it. Do it."

I become one with the rope and dagger. I'm no longer sweating. My pulse has settled. My breathing has calmed. I hear nothing. Feel no wind or sun.

The chants move into my fingers, behaving as twitches, faint notes of their usual selves.

I close my eyes. No need to look. I feel metal of my dagger blade pinched between my thumb and finger, feel my thumb and finger tips resting on rope. With my other hand on the handle, the dagger blade easily slides a small bit forward.

I stop.

I wait.

"Do it. Do it."

The dagger easily slides a small bit backwards.

I wait.

"Do it. Do it."

Forward.

"Do it. Do it."

Backwards.

Faster forward.

"Do it. Do it."

Faster backwards.

"You can do it. Just do it. Do it."

Wait! That isn't my chants. That's something else.

I look around.

"You can do it. Just do it. Do it."

It's the girl's voice.

"You can do it. Just do it. Do it."

The Girl Scout with the pink wagon.

"You can do it. Just do it. Do it."

I yell at air. "I already bought God-damn cookies from you. Leave me the fuck alone."

"You can do it. Just do it. Do it."

I scream, "Do what?"

My heartbeats are hastening. I'm shivering.

"You can do it. Just do it. Do it."

I stand and try to spear a pointed stray rock into a dusty spot of ground, but the dust is shallow. The rock bounces and bites my shin.

"God Almighty!"

"You can do it. Just do it. Do it."

"Quit saying that! I don't know what you want, little girl!"

She falls silent. Nowhere to be seen. Leaving me standing alone like an idiot, struggling to figure out what to do.

"You have sad eyes," she told me at the house.

What the hell did she mean?

"You're kind," she told me.

I scream again, "Are you memory or imagination or real or what, God damn it?"

But now her voice turns soft, a sweet whisper.

"Just do it."

Wind whirls around me and I know what she means.

Help Will enjoy what he's already loving.

I slide my dagger back into its sheath. I check the rope. It's minimally frayed. He won't notice. In my rucksack are the Lemon-Ups. I only ate two. The box is pretty much new, untouched.

I lay the Lemon-Ups box by the looped rope where Will can find them and know I was here. Cookies to celebrate his success when he climbs back on top.

I walk toward Mom's Prius.

"Do it. Do it," the chants sing.

I laugh and sing back, "I just did it, assholes."

Sun is warming me and wind is whistling happy tunes.
I faintly hear falcons sounding content.
I wonder how my eyes look. They feel less sad.
I did good. But it wasn't my doing. I'm not author.
I'm recipient.

DC Fidler (Author)

A native of the North Carolina Appalachian Mountains, DC Fidler has combined a career in academic psychiatry and cultural psychiatry with a lifetime of playwriting, acting, directing, composing music, and teaching creative writing and the dramatic arts.

He studied theatre, writing, medicine, and psychiatry at the University of North Carolina at Chapel Hill, where he served on the faculty. He later served on the faculty at West Virginia University and also practiced psychiatry in Australia and New Zealand.

He began his acting career in outdoor dramas, summer stock theatre, and local films and television at age ten. He has written scripts and composed music for over fifty medical educational videos and his plays have been produced in community theatres, at universities, and in professional theatres in North Carolina, Virginia, Ohio, West Virginia, Alaska, St. Louis, Sacramento, San Diego, Los Angeles, Boston, Chicago, and New York City.

He consulted and appeared in educational productions for HBO, ABC, and PBS and performed in stage plays including: *Hope is the Thing with Feathers, Night of January 16th, Thieves' Carnival, Blood Wedding, Our Town, A Life in the Theatre*, and *Fool for Love*. DC Fidler is an active member of the Dramatists Guild of America and the Charlotte Writers' Club.

Fidler previously chaired the Video Committee for the American Psychiatric Association and served as President of the Association for Academic Psychiatry, promoting the use of arts in psychiatry. He was inducted as a Fellow of the Royal College of Physicians of Ireland and serves on the Arts and Humanities Committee for the Group for the Advancement of Psychiatry, co-producing a video series on the History of Psychiatry.

DC Fidler lived and worked with the Alutiiq tribe in Akhiok, Alaska, the Al Moqbali Bedouin tribe near Sohar, Oman, the Kalkadoon Tribe in the outback of Queensland, Australia, and the Te Tau Ihu Maori Tribes on the South Island of New Zealand.

He is author of the textbook, *Psychiatry for Actors: Building a Character Using Psychiatric Principles*, and author of the novels, *Boogieban* and *Wood Whisperers*.

Plays, Novels, and Textbooks by DC Fidler

Novels and Textbooks
- Boogieban
- Wood Whisperers
- Psychiatry for Actors: Building a Character Using Psychiatric Principles

Plays
- Voices in the Woods
- Guilt by Association (With RJ Casey)
- Three Diaries
- Sir William Bowlinggreen and Company
- Shiraz
- Anniversary of Miss Nanette Pringle
- School Children Hiding Under Desks
- Grams
- Camp Uni
- Boogieban (Two-Actor Version)
- Boogieban (Seven-Actor Version)
- Ahulaqs
- Elk and Wolf (With Travis Teffner)
- Santee Delta (With Travis Teffner)
- Celtic Crossing
- Stone Touchin'
- Daugherty Park Merry-Go-Round
- La Dynastie
- The Last Farm
- Gyges
- Begat
- Hijacked Lives
- Five X

Short Plays
- Persons
- Cruise
- Mobile to Where
- Oman Truce
- Second Amendment
- The Greek God Club
- Microscopic Misconceptions
- Drone Guns
- Moon Bugs (With Travis Teffner)

Screenplays
- Green Lights of Baghdad (with RJ Casey)

Short Stories
- Recipient

Musicals
- Pied Piper (With Lauren Horacek)
- Healer Man
- Medicine Show